WAKING UP
An Unusual Transmigration

Margrit Goodhand

Therapy & Books
Dunedin, Florida

CW00435527

Live Your Potential

Waking Up: An Unusual Transmigration

Published by Therapy & Books

Dunedin, Florida

www.therapynbooks.com

Front cover Photography by Thomas Ackermann

ISBN (Paperback): 9780578990972

eISBN: 9780578990989

DEDICATION

This novella is dedicated to Markus, Carl, David, Dee, Sam, Lindsay, and Max, whom I love more than words can express.

Contents

ACKNOWLEDGEMENT

I would like to express my appreciation to Jennifer Sloane and John Whalen for their developmental edits, copy edits, and proofreading of my work. Further, I want to thank the members of the Dunedin Writers Group in Florida for their manuscript critiques during my work in progress. They continue to inspire me.

EPIGRAPH

As hunger and appetite propel us to find food, needs and curiosity drive scientists to explore new frontiers. Before all comes the faith that alleviating suffering, breaking barriers, and advancing the quality of life is possible.

~ Margrit Goodhand

PREFACE

I n this novella, I use experimental fiction to explore the metaphysical, reincarnation, and trauma. One of my goals was to show how a traumatized person might integrate her subjective and objective realities within a supportive environment. Alternate endings let the readers develop their own conclusions

Over the years, my clients came from all levels of society and ethnic-cultural backgrounds. They included professionals, the affluent, celebrities, the homeless, clergy, witches, warlocks, prostitutes, alcoholics, addicts, and the physically and mentally injured. Their common denominator was trauma.

As a clinical social worker/psychotherapist, I have learned to view my clients through a PIE (person-in environment) lens against historical backgrounds. It helps me to create interventions that relieve suffering. My adaptations of historical figures and events are designed to create such a background for the protagonist. Otherwise, all characters in my story are fictional

Waking Up: An Unusual Transmigration is perfect reading assignment for stimulating discussions in a behavioral science classroom or women's book club.

PROLOGUE

W hen Olivia meets Uri, a magical character, it challenges her existing paradigm of life. His knowledge of her unusual previous encounters contributes to Olivia's tentative acceptance of Uri's outrageous claims and promises. Subsequently, they develop a relationship that initiates her into the metaphysical.

Are Olivia's experiences figments of her imagination? Has she lost her mind? Or does she experience facets of soul transmigration, also known as reincarnation or gilgul? Is her life over, or will she discover a way to integrate her subjective experiences with her objective reality? These are some of the questions she struggles with during her fantastic excursions that the reader is invited to join.

A pivotal event sheds light on where Olivia finds herself and why. Options for alternate resolutions emerge, including a gender-specific intervention. This is Olivia's story.

CHAPTER ONE

The Soulmate

"May I sit at your table," a deep-timbered voice asks while Olivia is checking the e-mails on her tablet at Starbucks. She looks up—he had appeared out of nowhere. He seems familiar. *His green eyes sparkle like diamonds—yes, it was déjà vu.* He has an attractive Mediterranean appearance with bronze-toned skin. His black mid-length hair is curly-wavy with a stylish out-of-control flair. She quickly realizes that her blue eyes, fair skin, and blond shoulder-length hair provide an alluring visual contrast. *Opposites attract. The electromagnetic pull of emotion feels irresistible.*

"Sure," Olivia responds with a smile, already distracted from reading her e-mails because he definitely is more interesting. What had been an ordinary coffee shop was now transformed into a setting for a magical encounter. Out of the corner of her eye, Olivia watches as he places his cup on the table and slowly sits down. The nails of his long-fingered, strong hands are well-manicured.

"My name is Uri. I am your soulmate," he says matter-of-factly.

Shocked, Olivia looks up. She responds by gasping, "What?"

Uri nods his head a couple of times—as if what he said was normal—and reassures her in a comforting tone. "Yes, I really am."

Still baffled, Olivia stares at the handsome guy. Then she glances at her wedding band. A thought where Joe might be quickly flutters through her mind. Pursuing that thought would lead to a bottomless pit of speculation because there was no way to know his exact location.

Uri's lips are berry red. Between sips, he comments, "Mmm—I just love Frappuccino with mocha." He puts his right elbow on the table and rests his chin on his hand. While gazing at Olivia with amusement, he waits for her reaction.

He couldn't be real! But then, is this the Starbucks she went to twice a week? Today the atmosphere flickers with unusual specks of light, despite no sun shining through the windows. As Olivia straightens her back against the chair, she frantically considers her thoughts and options. *I could get up and leave, tell him to leave, or let him talk. He could be a psychopath, narcissist, or otherwise insane. Or perhaps he's just testing my reaction for his own reasons— like the two women from my past?* With both, Olivia had first thought they were crazy until they explained themselves. She decides to take a deep breath first to calm herself. Afterward, she takes a sip of her chai latte.

"Take your time," he calmly responds while opening the wrapper of his French madeleines and offering her one.

"No, thank you." She declines—despite madeleines being her favorite cookies.

"They're my favorite—after Turkish delights over the holidays," he says while nibbling on one, clearly enjoying the taste.

Incidentally, she also likes Turkish delights but chooses not to disclose it. Yet, she wonders what else they might have in common.

Her strange encounters with the two women from her past had occurred on separate occasions. The first was with Cindy, a supervisor. Impeccably groomed, with a mid-length platinum bob, and in her usual business attire, Cindy had expressed pride in being a "recovering codependent" during a weekly staff meeting while sitting across from Olivia. "I *really* like your two-toned earrings," she complimented her at the end of the meeting as their colleagues got up to leave.

"Thank you. I like them, too," Olivia said, feeling appreciated.

"May I have them?" Cindy asked without hesitation.

"What?" *Was she nuts?*

"I'll pay for them."

"I'm sorry, Cindy, but I just got these earrings yesterday. I like them too much." Cindy understood that Olivia meant it and let it go.

The following incident happened a week later during a dress-down Friday. Instead of jeans, Olivia had worn her low-cut yoga pants with a floral design, the ones she got at a five-dollar bargain at a yard sale. While sitting at her desk, Cindy approached her. "I *really* like your pants!" she said in a flattering tone.

"Thank you. I like them too." *Here we go again.*

"Where did you get them?"

"At my neighbor's yard sale. It was an excellent deal."

"May I have them?" This time Olivia wavered with her answer. I *wonder if she would pay me $10 for them. It's not that she is my friend whom I would just give my well-worn pants. She's a supervisor. In that position, she can easily afford that. And I could use the extra cash.*

"Sure, ten bucks, and they're yours," she answered, holding her breath.

"It's a deal!" Cindy's face lit up with delight.

"Great. I'll bring them on Monday after getting them washed."

"I can't wait. I like them a lot."

Only after the agreement, Cindy explained herself. "You know, I'm reading a book about getting what I want. One of my assignments is asking others to give me stuff that I like. The point is to see if I can get it but not take it personally if I can't. That's why I've been practicing with you. The first time I didn't get it, but this time I did. So, thank you. I appreciate it."

Olivia's most recent unusual encounter took place at a Publix grocery store in aisle two. An attractive, tanned woman in black slacks and a white blouse approached from the opposite direction pushing a shopping cart. Olivia had spotted her right after she had taken a big jar of Kosher Dill Pickles off the shelf and was about to place them into her own cart. Before they could pass each other, the woman stopped. Brightly smiling, she asked, "Hi, do you have a dollar?" as if it was the most normal thing to ask a stranger for money.

"What?" Olivia was shocked at the woman's audacity. Judging by her looks, she didn't need to panhandle. *What the heck would someone do with a single dollar anyway?*

"Do you have a dollar?" the woman repeated while sweeping the right side of her chin-length black hair behind her ear.

"Why?" Olivia countered. *What a nerve!* As she was still fishing for the right words to tell her to get lost, the woman continued.

"I'm working on becoming more successful in my business. That includes practicing to push boundaries by asking strangers for a dollar and feeling okay, despite what they may think about me. Men have been pushing boundaries for centuries because of male privilege, but as women, we have to learn it from scratch," she explained. Then she introduced herself, "My name is Mary. I own a bookstore up the road on 56th Street."

"Oh, thanks for clarifying. My name is Olivia," she replied while relaxing a bit. It started to make sense, especially in light of her earlier encounters with Cindy. *They must have read the same book.* "What you're doing is interesting. But, unfortunately, I don't carry cash today—I use my debit card to pay for groceries. Good luck getting your dollar, though."

"Thank you. It was nice talking to you. And thank you for not thinking I'm crazy—even though I don't really care," Mary said.

"Nice meeting you, too." Olivia laughed and then had an idea. She asked, "Do *you* have a dollar?"

"Sure, you want one?"

"Yes," she answered, curious to see if Mary would actually give it to her.

Surprisingly, she did. Olivia resisted the urge to tell her to keep it because she didn't need it either. Instead, she thanked her with a smile. After that, both went their separate ways and never met again.

Returning her attention to Uri, Oliva decides to let him talk. *If nothing else, at least an interesting story could come out of it—if I ever get around to writing one,* she thought.

"My name is Olivia. So, what do you want from me?"

Uri sips on his Frappuccino. "To get you ready for *everything*," he responds while studying her face.

"What is everything?"

"Everything you need to understand about yourself— your origins, why you are here, and your destiny. Are you interested?"

"How are you going to do that?" Olivia raises her eyebrows.

"By teaching you how to wake up in your dreams."

"I have no clue what that means."

"Let me explain: Waking up *in* a dream is different from waking up *from* a dream. After you master the former, you can learn to wake up in different time periods. But there's a learning curve to getting this; you have to practice. You must chant, 'Wake up in my dream' before falling asleep.

And, once you get that, we can meet *in* your dream instead of Starbucks next time, okay?"

"Oh, really?" Olivia replies with skepticism.

"Really! You pick a night. It can be any day during the week."

"Tuesday?" Olivia offers half-heartedly.

"Okay, sounds good."

"What time?"

"We don't have to set one. Remember to chant, 'Wake up in my dream' before falling asleep. Once lucid inside your dream, you can interact with the characters there to change its course toward a desired outcome. Alternately, you can also be asleep while you are awake. That is the sad case for most people. They think that what they see, hear, and feel in a limited reality is all that is to life."

"What do you mean?"

"Well, the reality is that people have been hypnotized by the glitter of all the stuff that is only temporary. And at the end of a life span— most have been indoctrinated to believe they only have *one* life—they have nothing to show that can raise them to a higher level in the next one. So then, they have to start all over again until getting it right.

"What is getting it right?"

"At one point, you will learn that after waking up in your past and future lives when fully awake," Uri responds.

"That makes perfect sense." Olivia replies sarcastically. Yet, she feels intrigued by this handsome guy and his outrageous claims. She looks at her wedding ring again. It does not stop her from feeling an irresistible pull toward Uri, who claims to be her soulmate.

Uri rises from his chair. His body movements are marked with virility. He picks up his cup and says with a mischievous smile, "Olivia, always remember that I am your soulmate. I was in many places with you while you were not conscious of me. There is a pattern that has prepared you for meeting me today. Remember those past encounters you had with Cindy and Mary?"

Olivia is stunned. Once able to respond, she asks, "How do you know about them?"

"Because I am your soulmate. As such, I share in the patterns that guide your life. First, with both women, you asked the question, 'What?' instead of walking away and then learned something important. Second, those encounters prepared you to meet me by asking the same question and getting to know yourself during our future adventures.

Intrigued, Olivia wants to know more. But before she can ask other questions, Uri has disappeared as mysteriously as he had appeared. She is left with pondering *Uri is a strange name*.

CHAPTER TWO

The Possibilities

A t bedtime, Olivia practices waking up in her dream. The first time, it does not work, and she has no idea what went wrong. She just falls asleep and wakes up in the morning. The second time, she remembers dreaming but accidentally tells herself to wake up *from* her dream. And she does—in her bed. After that, she goes to the refrigerator for a probiotic pineapple-yogurt. *It's bad to eat at night, but it's good for my digestive tract,* she rationalizes. After satisfying her cravings, she goes back to bed. The third time, it works like a charm, and she wakes up *in* her dream.

Olivia finds herself shopping at Fresh Market, looking for her favorite multigrain bread. Sadly, all the baskets with freshly baked goods are empty, and there is no one at the bakery counter. She feels disappointed because the Fresh Market is the only store where she buys bread. *Now I have to go to Publix*. Almost leaving the store without it, she remembers that she can change the outcome of her dream. It works, and she begins to redirect the events instead of leaving without getting what she came for.

She keeps looking for the store manager. Finally, she sees an employee near a cash register who wears slacks, a short-sleeved shirt, and a tie. Suspecting that he is the one in charge, she approaches him. "Hi. Are you the manager here?"

"Yes. How may I help you?" he responds politely.

"There is no one at the bakery counter. Would you please send someone to the back of the bakery to check for a fresh multigrain loaf?"

"Of course," he replies. "Staff to the baker counter, staff to the bakery counter," he announces over the loudspeaker. "Someone will be over shortly," he reassures her.

Olivia walks back to the bakery. Sure enough, the baker in a white jacket and hat has appeared. "Sorry, I was held up with cake decorations. What can I get you?"

"A loaf of fresh multigrain bread, sliced and double-bagged, please."

"Okay," he replies and begins to accommodate her request. He completes Olivia's order by fastening the inner and outer bags with twisty ties, adding a price label, and handing her exactly what she had requested.

###

Upon awakening, Olivia knows she is prepared to meet Uri. On the following day, a Tuesday, she goes to bed at 10:00 P.M. Before falling asleep, she chants, "Wake up in my dream." Excited at the prospect to meet her soulmate in this manner, Olivia has difficulty falling asleep. When she finally drifts off, she dreams about a turkey that hides in a pumpkin field to escape becoming the victim of a meal. She relates it to Thanksgiving and her recent choice not to eat poultry any-more. Because there is no Uri, she commands herself, "Wake up in my dream to meet Uri!" To her surprise, it works.

Olivia finds herself sitting on a swivel chair at a table in a dine-in movie theater. Shortly after, Uri appears out of the blue—just like before at Starbucks. He wears striped slacks and a deep red polo shirt that enhances the green of his eyes. Today, she is not preoccupied with reading the emails on her laptop. She expects the continuation of an exciting conversation. Her entire focus is on Uri as he steps to the side of the table to greet her.

She notices that he is intensely present during their interactions. *His emotional intelligence matches his physical attractiveness*. Rising from her chair, Olivia says, "I can't believe this really worked."

"Hi Olivia, I'm glad it did," he replies, softly touching her shoulders, and lightly kissing her on both cheeks. It feels right. Then they both sit down.

After exchanging initial niceties, she asks him about the plan for today.

"Well, we could start with looking at your past lives," Uri suggests.

"What if I don't believe in that stuff?" Olivia asks. Then, she quickly adds, "And even if I had any, I don't remember any of them."

"That's because you were sleepwalking until now. But, because I was awake, I can take you there—just take your pick."

"What do you mean? There are options?"

"Let's see—your advanced genotype is mostly Southeastern European, followed by Western European, South Asian, and minor American admixtures, we can pick from that. Alternately, we can go as far as the Mitochondrial Eve in Kenya."

"Wow, really?"

"Really!"

"That's incredible. I only knew about ancestors from Eastern and Western Europe.

"Locations don't mean anything because they are fabricated. They are part of the glitter that changes or disappears, depending on who is sitting on the turf and rules. It's the relationships that count in the world of souls."

"That's interesting, but why haven't we met before?"

"Because I can only be around for you when you are awake in your dreams."

"Like now?"

"Yes, like now."

"But what happened at Starbucks? Was I asleep then?"

"At Starbucks, you were in the twilight and ready to wake up. Because soulmates are magical, they introduce themselves only in the twilight and when a person is ready for initiation to the formerly unknown."

"Oh, okay. But there are so many past life options to choose from. What do you recommend?"

"That's totally up to you. It will come to you by the next time we meet."

"How do you know?"

"Because it will come to you from the source deep within. It's the only thing that means anything. The outside is all glitter that will go away."

"I can't say I understand completely."

"Do you want to try waking up in a past life?"

"Sure."

"Excellent. Let's meet again soon."

"Okay, where?"

"In your past life. The details as to the place for our meeting will emerge."

"Okay. I guess I will have to trust you."

"Be assured that you can. I promise. We will go on many adventures together, and I will be with you every step of the way even though you might not recognize me like now."

"What does that mean?"

"Well, I am part of you. I only step in when needed to aid you in other realms. However, you must know that I have lived past lives as well."

"Hmm. Will I know you when I see you in one?"

"Perhaps. But at the least, you'll have hunches."

Before leaving, Uri kisses her lightly on both cheeks again. Then, with a mischievous smile, he offers his own cheeks to Olivia. He points at them with his right index finger. By now, Olivia feels more relaxed in his presence and responds in kind.

"That's funny." She laughs. "I like this kissing on the cheeks ritual, although it's new to me."

"You did it quite regularly during your past life in France," he clarifies. Then he turns around and disappears, leaving Olivia behind in the theater.

While puzzled by that comment, Olivia feels more interested in her Southeastern origins. Specifically, she wants to explore a past life—if there was one—in the Balkans She is curious how she would meet Uri there. He said that, at the least, she would have hunches.

Suddenly, the giant movie screen comes alive. White letters begin to form words until the phrase *Into the Past* blazes against a starry sky. Then, the theater fills with the bright sounds of expressive Turkish dance music in a Kalisama irregular beat and rhythm. A Tarbur reed flute beckons with longing for answers, while a Ney string instrument responds with gentleness and determination. As a Kas cymbal affirms and emphasizes a perfect union, the white letters and black sky turn into a spiral and pull Olivia into the past.

She finds herself standing in a row, among six bearded Sufi dervishes in black robes and long brown hats. They remove their black garments and place them on the floor— revealing white robes underneath. After that, they cross their arms and respectfully bow in unison. Instinctively, Olivia knows what to do. Prompted by the cymbal, she steps in, joining the dervishes as they take turns whirling onto the dance floor until forming a circle. As their speed increases, they raise their arms until their hands touch their shoulders. Then, at full pace, they whirl with outstretched arms like wings. Their gazes are turned inward. Faster, faster, faster... until Olivia feels herself spinning—into the Ottoman Empire.

CHAPTER THREE

1532 CE – Inside the Topkapi Palace, Istanbul

O livia is standing at the palace kitchen counter, waiting for a tray. Her name is Meryem, and she has no memory of her life as Olivia. Next to her is Kismet, the tall *Kapi Agha* (head eunuch) faking a frown. Jokingly, he moves his right hand over his neck. The gesture signals Nasuh, the head chef behind the counter, that he will get beheaded unless he quickly produces the tray with afternoon refreshments for Hurrem, the Sultan's favorite. Meryem picks up a tray with fresh fruit, Turkish delights, and pomegranate ginger sorbet every afternoon around the same time for Hurrem.

"Hurry, hurry, hurry!" Kismet orders impatiently in his high-pitched voice. He nods his head wrapped in a multi-colored turban and flaps his hands like bird's wings. Kismet's demeanor shows that he is used to giving orders to Nasuh, the chef with a chubby face who wears a white-bordered ochre-colored cap.

"It's coming, it's coming, it's coming," replies Nasuh hurriedly with a subservient smile. Then, in an exaggerated fashion, he bows in the direction of Kismet as if he were the Sultan himself, who, in contrast to his subjects, rarely smiles and whose stature and controlled demeanor is one of a noble person and fierce warrior.

Meryem enjoys watching the daily drama between her two friends. She especially finds it entertaining when they insult each other accompanied by lively gestures. Thankfully, it had not yet come to a fistfight. When Kismet tries to boss her around like that, she replies in kind, which he seems to enjoy. Last night she had dreamt that she was his wife and that they made love after passionately quarreling, which was utterly ridiculous. As a fully castrated eunuch, he is physically unable to have intercourse and legally forbidden to engage in other intimacies with the women in the palace.

Meryem's birth name had been Miriam before entering the imperial harem. Slaves could have slaves, and she was assigned to Hurrem, whose birth name was Aleksandra, historically known by her Turkish nickname Roxelana. Both fair-skinned, with full heads of long hair, and without visible flaws, they had been bought for top liras. As a sign of their status in the palace, a pointed hat with gold embroidery tops Hurrem's strawberry red hair whereas Meryem's light blonde hair is capped by a short cylinder with stripes. Both headpieces have ultra-thin veils that fall to the back but can also be used to cover faces.

Miriam and Aleksandra had been kidnapped from their village by Crimean Tartars. While on the slave ship on the way to Istanbul, Aleksandra remained defiant—even after the beatings with wet rags that hurt but left no bruises on her voluptuous body so that she could be sold at full value. Instead of eating the food offered by the guards, she tried to jump off the boat.

"I will rather die in the sea. Let me die in the sea!" Aleksandra had screamed over and over during a violent storm as she struggled to jump into the roaring waves. She was in severe shock after witnessing her parents and fiancée getting massacred in the Greek Orthodox church where her father had been the priest, and the villagers had sought shelter during the raid. Those who had not died during the massacre perished in the fire set by the raiders.

"I will not let you die! We will survive this together," Miriam had shouted tirelessly, almost falling overboard herself while not only fighting against the forceful winds but also a heavier body to prevent the suicide. Finally, Aleksandra gave up and safely collapsed in her arms.

During a brief separation, they were examined like cattle, packaged in transparent garments, and adorned with cheap jewelry that enhanced their nakedness. After that, they were forced to parade at the Suleiman Pasa Han Slave Market until bought for the imperial harem at the Topkapi Palace. After their conversions, Aleksandra's name was changed to Hurrem—a term of endearment related to whore, and Miriam's name to Meryem. In a brief period of time, Hurrem rose to become the sultan's favorite consort and Meryem to the role of her most loyal slave.

No one else at the palace knew that they had grown up together in the same family, a fact they had sworn to take to their graves so no one could ever use it against them. By now, Meryem had seen too often how the vicious fights among harem factions over privileges and benefits had produced deadly outcomes, regardless of status. She frowned as she struggled to understand and reconcile the following: *I live in a harem, a designated zone in which specific conduct or access by certain individuals is forbidden. Ironically, the word harem also describes the interior of a mosque, the sacred compound in Jerusalem, and the holy cities of Mecca and Medina.*

"All done, Meryem, take it." Nasuh places the large tray with the afternoon refreshments on the counter. As usual, he hands Kismet a small bowl of extra Turkish delights. In turn, Kismet offers one to Meryem, who utters an enthusiastic "Mmm" while chewing the nutty part of the candy and letting the rest of the sugar-dusted cube melt on her palate until ready to swallow it all.

"That's so you don't steal from the tray and get in big trouble," the head eunuch snarls at her, shaking his head and rolling his eyes, but his face shows obvious affection.

"Thank you, Kismet, the most generous of all Sultan's servants," Meryem responds, also shaking her head and rolling her eyes back at him.

"May Allah bless you," Kismet replies, waving her away and adding, "Go, go, go!"

She picks up the tray, briefly bows, smiles, and leaves the kitchen, walking towards the third courtyard, which is the site of the royal family and the imperial harem. Moving along the intricate mosaic floor tiles through the labyrinth of hallways, she passes walls decorated with ornamental tiles and precious wood carvings. There are stone pillars so thick that one can fully hide behind them to spy on someone.

On her way to Hurrem's quarters, Meryem passes a group of women who wear *salvars* (harem pants) like hers. Their blouses have hanging sleeves and are topped with vests. All heads are covered, but their faces are not veiled. While walking along the hallway, the sultan's delicate wife Madeira and her stocky henchwoman Hira approach from the opposite direction. Their sinister glances show open contempt for Meryem, who must remain polite because of her subordinate status.

"Sultana," Meryem says while stopping in her tracks and bowing respectfully. All female relatives of the sultan had to be addressed and greeted as *Sultana*, which means strength and authority. Aside from evil looks, Madeira and Hira refuse any response. Just after they pass, Hira takes two steps back and turns at a 90-degree angle. "Sssss!" she hisses at Meryem, exposing her canines and fangs. She intentionally bumps hard into Meryem with her right shoulder and then elbows her in the side. The tray with the refreshment slips out of Meryem's hands, and everything crashes on the marble floor. Meryem barely catches herself from falling backward. She is shocked into the realization that her sense of relief had been premature. Thinking that both had already passed, she had been unprepared to protect herself against the assault.

Thankfully, nothing worse happens this time. Meryem returns to the kitchen to arrange for the cleanup of the mess and get a second tray. After they find out what happened, Nasuh and Kismet openly curse Madeira and Hira. As Nasuh provides Meryem with a new tray of refreshments, he whispers in her ear, "I will spit in the sherbets they ordered for later," which makes Meryem laugh. And when Kismet gives her one of his magical amulets to protect her from the evil eye, she feels empowered.

Carrying a new tray of refreshments and armed with the amulet hidden inside her décolleté, Meryem walks down the hallway again. Despite holding on to the idea that the talisman will protect her, a concern about what evil deed Madeira might be planning next remains. When she finally arrives at the stairway leading to the second floor without further incidents, she takes a breath of relief. As usual, she looks forward to exchanging the palace news with her friend. *By now, everyone knows that at the order of Suleiman, his concubine Hurrem has been freed and is no longer a slave like his wife, Madeira. And that to the disdain of his mother Hafsa, Suleiman has become monogamous with Hurrem. As a result, Hafsa has become unable to uphold the order of the harem by manipulating sexual appetites and salaries. The women are out of control.*

Neither Madeira nor any of Suleiman's concubines have walked the golden road to his chamber since his brief affair with the Castilian Princess Isabella. After Turkish pirates had kidnaped Isabella and her servants, they were sold to Suleiman, who started liking her too much. As a result, Hurrem and her friends had been in great danger. Fortunately, Meryem was able to implement Hurrem's plan to end the affair and get the princess eliminated with the aid of Kismet and Nasuh.

The situation had demanded swift and ruthless action to prevent all of them from being assassinated first so Isabella and her favorites would not replace them. Getting rid of her was the only way to make it possible for Suleiman and Hurrem to continue a passionate relationship that included reading and writing poetry to each other.

As per Hafsa, there can only be one explanation that has spread like wildfire, "Hurrem has bewitched the sultan with forbidden spells."

CHAPTER FOUR

Challenging the Dynasty

M eryem arrives at Hurrem's chamber. One of two tall eunuchs standing guard knocks at the door for her.

"Come in," Hurrem commands, expecting the afternoon refreshments.

The eunuch opens the door, and Meryem enters.

"Vaseki," Meryem respectfully bows using the customary greeting for 'favorite' in relationship to the sultan. Then she proceeds to place the tray on the round table designed for snacks.

Hurrem is sitting on a diwan. As usual, she wears a pointed headdress adorned with jewels on her forehead. A flowing turquoise garment of silk partially covers a white salvar gathered around the ankles. The turquoise enhances her red hair. As she signals the guard with her right hand, he moves several steps back, still facing her. Then he bows, turns around, and leaves the chamber.

This is the opportunity for Hurrem and Meryem to spend time alone. The children are taking their afternoon naps in the annexing chamber while another slave watches them.

Upon awakening, they will join them for refreshments. In the meantime, Hurrem and Meryem engage in one of their heart-to-heart conversations. Typically, they are meaningful and characterized by the shared sorrow of having been violently uprooted and subjugated.

"I thought they would kill me right then and there." Meryem sighs after telling Hurrem the story of the encounter in the hallway with Hurrem's rival Madeira and her slave Hira who does all the dirty work for her.

"They would not dare. I will make sure of that," replies Hurrem hugging her loyal friend, who ironically has become her own slave. "They will pay for this," she adds, providing Meryem with the support she so desperately needs. "I plan to become the Sultan's legal wife. That will put me another step above Madeira, who is still a slave despite being married to him. Unlike her, I'm already free, but after marrying him, I will become Hurrem Sultana," she states with confidence.

"Hurrem! How would that be possible? It has never been done before." Meryem's eyes open widely.

"Suleiman has never freed any of his previous concubines either. Yet here I am, a free woman allowed to engage in charity work," she explains. "And he has been monogamous for years now, although it upsets his mother and the order of the harem. He would rather read Rumi and his own poetry to me than get involved with anyone else.

And thanks to your help, the only threat to our positions is at the bottom of the sea."

With a smile, Hurrem proceeds to show Meryem a selection of poetry the sultan had composed under his pen name Muhibbi. Meryem's eyes widen as she reads *Thone of my lovely niche, my wealth, my love, my moonlight....* Meryem gasps for air and comments, "You are breaking barriers."

"You haven't seen anything until I get him to marry me," Hurrem holds her head high. "That is because Suleiman loves me, and I have learned to love him. But, my dear friend, the day will come when you can get out of here as a free woman and can marry whomever you want."

Could it be? Meryem wonders, contemplating the idea of freedom for herself. She would do anything for Hurrem now because their dreams are linked. Her mind wanders to the past. As the child of a Jewish merchant killed on the Silk Road that linked China to the West, she had been adopted by a Ruthenian Greek Orthodox couple who raised her as Christian after her mother had died. Now, she finds herself stuck in the Topkapi Palace with the daughter of a Greek Orthodox priest. But there is Jakuv from the jewelry shop at the market who makes her heart pound. She blushes as she remembers the promising words of the numerologist she had consulted for an entire month of her salary.

CHAPTER FIVE

Breaking Through

S ultan Suleiman the Magnificent marries Hurrem in 1533 CE at a spectacular ceremony. But unfortunately, the marriage is an insult to the existing dynasty, and Hurrem's enemies begin to revolt. It starts with an attack in open daylight on her trusted slave Kismet at the market while he is shopping for spices. Kismet is unprepared to face an ever-growing mob encircling him suddenly—there is no avenue for escape.

"He is with the witch!" "Shame on you!" "Die, eunuch, die!" Kismet hears the voices of the mob scream insults and painfully feels their blind attacks with fists, feet, and any objects they can lay their hands on.

Subjected to a bombardment of punches and kicks, Kismet is abandoned to powerlessness. It does not stop after he is pushed on the ground, hitting his head on a stone. Instead, a demon with many faces continues to inflict pain until he loses consciousness, with his mind dissociating from this reality but connecting to deeply buried events within from the past. By the time the guards intervene, he is unaware that they are transporting him back to the palace. Meryem hears of the tragic event when returning the empty tray to the kitchen. After looking for him, she finds her battered and bruised friend fading in and out of awareness while the palace physician attends to him.

"No, no, no!" Kismet screams while squirming on the bed, tortured by flashbacks. "Help! I want to go home—Mama, Papa, Mama, Papa, help, help!" he screams and groans. He relives how he, as the eight-year-old Atanas, had been kidnapped by two bearded Coptic monks. One offers him candy with a smile while he is playing with his friends in the village square. As soon as he walks over to accept it, the vultures in their black garbs snatch him and haul him off to the Abou Gerbe Monastery.

Kismet's excruciating physical pain at the monastery has resurfaced. It links to the pain he feels in the present; he re-experiences the trauma of being bound to a special chair, gagged by a piece of cloth in his mouth, legs forced apart, limbs securely tied, and utterly helpless. At the same time, one of the monks fastens a tight rope around his genitals. Out of the right corner of his eye, he sees a fiery glowing blade, and then—in a flash, his entire physical manhood is gone with a single stroke, followed by the jamming of a goose quill into his urethra. The wound is sealed with boiling oil and sand applied to catch any bleeding. The demon of pain devours him until he is carried away by mercifully angelic wings of unconsciousness.

The boy is feverish upon awakening. Immersed to the hips in a cold-water pool amidst the grass, he feels excruciating pain not only at the site of his amputation but also radiating throughout his entire being. Without choice, he joins an involuntary circle of moaning and screaming from other boys, the hellish opposite of the sound of cultured music. Fading in and out of awareness, he loses all concept of time. Occasionally monks come to check on him and the other wretches. Periodically, they lift the boys out of the water to drag them to a nearby mass grave or the recovery hall. He is selected for the latter.

In the recovery hall, he is not yet out of danger. His fever is waxing and waning slowly like the moon with periods of complete darkness. He overhears the monks talking about the possibilities for his future. As a child, he has no idea what either of these options mean. And, as a victim, he has no choice in the matter. Over the next couple of weeks, he learns that he is not suited to undergo formal training to sing in the popular staged music or drama of the Composite Monarchies. As a full castrato who had both testicles and penis removed, he has no genital to allow for sexual exploitation; therefore, he is better suited to become a eunuch for a harem. As a result, he is shipped to

Istanbul. There he is bought by the grand vizier and begins his upwardly mobile career path, eventually becoming the head eunuch in the Topkapi Palace.

Over the years, Atanas forgets who he is—like countless uprooted Ottomans. He becomes Kismet, who lives and works in a palace surrounded by luxury, enjoying the finest that life has to offer to a eunuch. And he wields tremendous power as the primary guardian over the harem. Until now. The past and the present have begun to merge; they leave no space for the possibility of a future he can be part of. Not only is he tortured by memories of the mind but also by ones of the body that cut deep into the core of his being and radiate into each cell—there was no escape from this. During the next few weeks, Kismet's body heals from the wounds of the mob attack, but his mind and emotions remain part of a bleeding river that cannot be seen by the eyes.

Meryem brings the news of Kismet's attack to Hurrem's attention. Periodically, she checks on him and reports to Hurrem on his status. Finally, when the time seems right and the physician approves, Hurrem visits Kismet. She is shocked to witness the absolute defeat of what, in the past, had been a cheerful personality. After she starts a conversation, he answers each of her questions out of respect but monotonously. But when she addresses him as Kismet, he responds with fierce determination.

"I am Atanas, not Kismet. I cannot come to terms with what has happened to me. I had loving parents, brothers, and sisters and came from a village in Greece where everybody knew my name. Then, after taking one piece of candy, they took my manhood, and I became a nobody. Since then, the demon of pain has taken over and condemned me to silence. Now he is telling me who I really am, what happened to me, and that there is no hope for someone like me."

Attentively, Hurrem listens to him and finds the meaning behind his words—after all, they had been bought at the same slave market before coming to the palace. Kismet's body language, facial expression, and eyes tell more than his words ever could. She grasps that she holds a key of life and death over this amazing man who has proven his loyalty to her over and over. It is time to act as both Hurrem and Aleksandra to stop the bleeding.

"Here is what I will do for you," she says firmly.

Kismet does not respond, his flat affect and silence giving away his hopeless state.

"I am setting you free. As of today, you are no longer a slave," she adds with authority tempered by compassion and without having consulted with anyone else.

"Sultana?" Kismet responds, his face showing signs of life with a mixture of disbelief and surprise.

CHAPTER SIX

THE POWER OF COFFEE
AND CHARITY

After the executioner beheads the leaders of the attack against Kismet, it becomes safe for him to be out in public again. At first, he is lost, not knowing what to do with his newfound freedom. Then, while looking at fabrics at the market, he meets Adom, a slim darker-skinned eunuch from Egypt dressed in elegant attire and turban. Instantly, they become best friends. Adom, also a full castrato, introduces him to Arabica beans, their fine grinding, and boiling the grounds in long-handled copper or brass pots to brew and serve kaveh (coffee). Kismet knows that once the palace embraces the new custom, kaveh will become popular enough to be sold to the public.

Finally, the day has come to meet with Nasuh and Meryem in the palace kitchen. Kismet introduces them to the beans and needed utensils to grind and cook the kahve, just as he had learned from Adom. After his friends are captivated by the aroma, their initial skepticism gives way to curiosity and an eagerness to taste it. Kismet fills a small porcelain cup with the foamy brew and takes a sip. "Hmm—it sharpens the mind and increases vitality."

"Really? Let me try. I need a boost of energy," Meryem responds as the scent caresses her olfactory sense. Kismet pours cups for her and Nasuh. While both of their faces show an aversion to the bitterness of kaveh, they agree on feeling energized shortly after drinking it.

Kismet has already provided the Sufi dervishes with a steady supply of Arabica beans; the consumption of kaveh allows them to swirl quickly through the night before crashing in the early morning. As typical with survivors of severe oppression and wounding, Kismet's aspirations have merged with his economic and spiritual needs. Now it is time to introduce the brown gold to Hurrem. With the support of Hurrem and the sultanate, his wholesale purchase of Arabica beans could potentially launch lucrative trade agreements. That, and selling them to retailers at the market for sale to the public would undoubtedly enrich the treasure chest of the sultanate.

It is time for Hurrem's afternoon snacks. Today, Kismet accompanies Meryem; he carries the second tray with kaveh in a shiny copper cezve and a small colorful porcelain cup. As usual, Meryem places the refreshments on the large table in front of the divan while Kismet puts his tray on a side table. Hurrem is eager to test the kaveh's energizing effect.

"Mmm, it smells delicious. I want to try it before anything else," Hurrem requests with anticipation.

"Yes, Sultana." Kismet carefully pours the kaveh into the cup and brings it to her. "While it's not sweet, one gets used to the taste. It's definitely worth the experience of mental alertness after a few minutes of drinking it," he explains. Attentively, both he and Meryem wait for Hurrem's reaction.

After taking a sip, Hurrem frowns. "It smells good, but it's bitter." In a surprise move, she takes a piece of Turkish Delight covered with powdered sugar and drops it into the cup. Then she tries again. "There, much better," she says with a smile.

After Hurrem verifies that kaveh lives up to its reputation, she introduces it to the sultan. As a result, it becomes a regular staple in the palace. The news of the therapeutic effect of the beverage spreads quickly, and kaveh gains increasing popularity with the people. Kismet is given the authority to set up and monitor the supply channels for the new demand of Arabica beans. Coffeehouses spring up everywhere. Suddenly, individuals from diverse backgrounds, who otherwise would not have mingled, start exchanging ideas on life and voicing opinions on social and political activity.

Because the social status lines become blurry during the late-night gatherings in the coffeehouses, it changes the way people relate to each other. Also, men are away from their families instead of being at home. Soon, the religious leaders blame kaveh for disrupting the social order. Then talks of independence become a threat to upholding the dynasty's foundation. By the time the highest-ranking cleric Bostanzade Mehmet Efendi bans coffee, it is too late. People in and out of the palace are addicted to caffeine and a new way of life. No matter what, they continue to drink kaveh. And Kismet, in addition to being free, has become a wealthy man enjoying his partnership with Adom.

By now, Hurrem has forged alliances with powerful dignitaries in the empire to create the *Istanbul Charitable Foundation* that serves the poor by opening a soup kitchen and a school. They become the first among others to follow. Because she needs a trusted righthand to oversee the establishment, she sets Meryem free, so she can do the charity work that, as a slave, would be forbidden to her.

One day, Meryem dares to walk into the jewelry store at the market where Jakuv, whom she likes, sits behind the counter. A necklace with a Star of David pendant, among other jewelry, catches her eye. Having a generous and well-deserved salary, she now has the money to buy whatever she wants. She senses a magnetic pull towards Jakuv. Her heart flutters every time she looks in his direction.

Jakuv's Mediterranean origins are apparent. His skin is bronzed, and his curly-wavy black hair shows partially beneath an embroidered Kavase cap. Familiar with fabrics worn by Sephardic Jews, Meryem notices that underneath a well-tailored djubba robe, he wears a striped inner cloak made of silk with golden embroidery fastened by a belt. His eyes are diamond green and sparkle. They remind her of someone she cannot remember.

"What a beautiful necklace. I remember my mother having one almost like that," she says—opening the door to a conversation about families.

"Your mother was Jewish? What happened?" Jakuv asks in a deep-timbered voice that sounds oddly familiar. *Déjà vu again.* His facial expression shows intense interest. *Opposites attract*, she thinks aware of her contrasting light skin and blonde hair—the latter covered with a pastel-colored silk scarf with floral design. Feeling comfortable in his presence, Olivia feels safe enough to divulge details of her life history.

"Both of my parents were Karaite Jews. They died when I was five years old. My father was murdered on the silk road to China when it was forbidden to travel there, and my mother died from consumption. I was adopted and raised by Greek-Orthodox parents until they were killed by Crimean slave traders who abducted me. But Hurrem set me free so that I could do charity work. I still live at the palace. And you? What about your family?"

"My parents were killed in the Spanish Inquisition. After their forced conversions, they secretly continued their Jewish practices, for which they were labeled as marranos, meaning swine, and brutally murdered. My older brother and I had a chance to flee to Istanbul where we can openly remain Jewish but have to pay the Jizya tax," Jakuv answers with sadness on his face.

"We are both orphans then," she notes with a faint smile feeling tears welling in her eyes.

"I guess you're right. I have seen you before, and I liked you then," he replies, also smiling. "What is your name?"

"Meryem. I always liked peeking through your window. In the past, I could only afford window shopping. Today, I can afford to buy something. How much is the necklace?"

"The necklace is already yours, and you don't owe me anything," Jakuv says firmly.

"That is so very generous of you." Meryem could barely believe what she heard. "Your name is Jakuv, right?"

"Yes, and you, Meryem, will never have to pay for anything I give you from my store."

"Why?"

"Because no matter what, we are already family!"

CHAPTER SEVEN

Choosing the Or

*W*hy am I back home after living as Meryem in the Topkapi Palace? I am trapped in psychosis with bizarre hallucinations. This will not end well because I am married to Joe, but my soulmate is Uri—that is if Uri actually exists. Olivia ponders what to do. She contemplates talking to Sandy, her yoga teacher; Fred, the psychiatrist at work; or Patel, her primary doctor from India.

She heard all three making statements before that they believe in reincarnation. *Because I feel so close to her, could it be that I am Meryem incarnated? And is Uri Jakuv? She is almost certain of it. Yet, it is one thing to believe in reincarnation and another one to actually experiencing it.* Olivia suspects that Sandy would tell her to see someone like Fred. But first, she would have to see Patel for a referral so her insurance would pay for it. After that, she'd end up with involuntary hospitalization for a mental health examination followed by court-ordered treatment with antipsychotics. In the end, she'd wind up with irreversible drooling and a shuffling walk. In short, her career as a therapist would be ruined.

Olivia can't help but laugh at the irony of life. She never took any of the three of them seriously. And now—if *they* knew what she is going through, the tables would surely be turned. She has another thought of talking to a priest but quickly decides against it. Traditional Christianity allows for one incarnation that has already taken place and a resurrection to come. That leaves absolutely no acceptable room to explain what she is going through. There seems to be no way out.

The following Tuesday, Olivia goes to bed again at 10:00 PM. She plans to meet Uri in a dream to discuss her concerns. *I am like an addict who asks her drug dealer for help with her addiction.* Before falling asleep, she chants like before, "Wake up in my dream."

It works, and like before, she finds herself sitting on a swivel chair in the dine-in theater. Today, whining sounds of a shofar and intermittent Hebrew chants fill the room. The screen populates letters, words, and sentences from the right to the left that Olivia cannot read. After a few moments, Uri shows up. Again, he walks over to her chair and greets her with a brief hug and kisses on both cheeks. She responds in kind.

"Hi, Olivia, it's good to see you," he says, looking straight into her eyes.

As when they first met, she notices that Uri's eyes are green—just like Jakuv's in the Ottoman Empire, who had shown her the same type of affection. Suddenly, it dawns on her that they could be the same soul living in different bodies—like herself and Meryem. That thought is at once followed by *someone needs to lock me up and throw away the key.*

"I know what you're thinking," says Uri, making matters worse.

"What!" she shouts. *This is getting more insane by the minute.*

"That I might be the soul living in the person you met in your past life."

"How do you know?"

"Because I have been asking myself the same question until I knew for sure."

"What question?"

"For example, if you, Olivia, have been the Meryem in one of my pasts when I was Jakuv."

"That's crazy. I am not in any type of reality that makes sense right now. You got me to think that I woke up in a dream. Reality—I don't even know what that is anymore. I feel trapped in a psychosis with delusions and bizarre hallucinations. I am either the schizophrenic or your co-schizophrenic sharing your sickness."

"That's one way to put it!" Uri laughs. "Or—"

"Or what?" Olivia interrupts him.

"Gilgul is really happening."

"What in the world is gilgul?"

"It means 'wheel' and is another word for soul transmigration or reincarnation."

"Oh," Olivia says as if now he made sense but immediately regrets it.

"Let's talk to the Rav, okay?"

"Who?" she gasps.

Uri laughs. "The Rav." He carefully pronounces the word and then explains, "A rav is a teacher, similar to a rabbi or rebbe. The one I know has not only the education but also actual experiences in matters of reincarnation. So perhaps he can explain what's going on."

"Of course, the Rav." Olivia's answer is loaded with cynicism.

"His name is Shlomo Finkelstein. He lives near the beach." Uri responds with a smile.

"And I am delusional and have bizarre hallucinations," she chuckles.

"I will schedule an appointment. Meet me at Starbucks next Tuesday around noon. After coffee, we go see the Rav, yes?"

Olivia thinks this might be against her better judgment, but there is also a small chance that Uri could be right. At least she would see him again at Starbucks this time instead of getting only hunches of him in a past life. There is no one else she can talk to about what she is going through—except the Rav. And, if she has lost her mind, then she has nothing else to lose anyway.

"This is probably nuts—but let's go," she hears herself agreeing.

CHAPTER EIGHT

With the Rav

R av Shlomo lives near the bay in a flood-safe house built upon tall posts. There is a large fenced-in pool in the back with two huge pipes and a filtering system connected to the saltwater. Uri leads the way to the entrance, which the Rav leaves unlocked for visitors he knows. After entering a foyer, Uri and Olivia step into a hallway and see an open door. Shlomo is standing behind an adjustable standing desk in a spacious home office. Upon seeing Uri and Olivia, he closes his laptop, and his face brightens with a smile.

"Hello Uri and friend, it's good to see you. Please, sit and make yourselves comfortable." The Rav points to a dark-stained bamboo seating arrangement in the left corner. Two walls are entirely covered by wooden bookshelves filled with weighty tomes. Against another wall is a long cabinet; on its counter are a Keurig, SodaStream Fizzy, cups, and tray with napkins and other incidentals. After Uri introduces Olivia, they all sit down.

Uri had first met Shlomo in a Walgreen's parking lot when he had a flat tire. The Rav had given him his own spare that fit. That day had marked the beginning of a friendly mentor-mentee relationship.

"Olivia, I'm so glad you came," the Rav says with a smile and asks her to explain what is bothering her.

Overcoming a fleeting impulse to run, she decides to stay. Encouraged by the Rav, she begins to share her experiences. When she gets stuck, he encourages her to continue. He reminds her of a good-natured wizard. His face is oval-shaped, friendly, and tanned. His sky-blue eyes are topped by thick black eyebrows frosted with a touch of grey. A black beret tops long strands of silvery hair, and a same-colored beard reaches down to his chest. He wears a black vest over a slightly wrinkled white linen shirt with matching long pants. Framed diplomas cover an entire wall. Olivia notices that he holds doctorate degrees in Ontology, Psychology, and Law. As per Uri, some think he is a Tzaddikim (Righteous One) with the widest knowledge and deepest wisdom while others consider him an incorrigible heretic.

Shlomo loves visitors. While his education has helped him develop a keen insight into personalities and their unique characters, he now views humans primarily as souls. He has embraced all opposites in that he views them as two sides of one coin instead of being mutually exclusive. And, after spending three years in the mystical city of Safed in Israel, he decided that he would earn his livelihood without using religious texts as tools of his trade. He attentively listens to Olivia.

Now more than ever, Shlomo is convinced that his mission is to make himself useful as souls reach out to him. From his experiences, he has learned that no preparation for meeting with the souls is needed; solutions to problems always arise during the interactions. As souls weave in and out of his life, he provides guidance and sometimes practical assistance—regardless of financial, religious, or irreligious status.

"If you could sum up your problem in one sentence, what would it be?" he asks Olivia with a sincere look.

"That I have gone insane because I no longer know what is real and what not.

"Is that all?" the Rav laughs. "Would you please give me an example?"

"Yes. I recently woke up in a previous life in the Ottoman Empire. Uri tells me he knows me from there when he was Jakuv, the jeweler with whom I had fallen in love there. He also tells me that he is my soulmate. I have no clue what any of that means."

"Thank you, Olivia. I am confident that we can clear all that up. But the most critical issue is to firmly establish what sanity is, so you can benefit from it in the present—wherever you find yourself. Agreed?"

"Agreed—because I don't want to end up in a psych ward."

"I can't blame you, and I can promise you that won't happen."

"Really?"

"Really."

Suddenly, a slim, midsize woman wearing a red-and-gold kaftan with a matching knot-design turban enters the room. She carries a tray filled with fresh fruit and pastries. With a smile and a cheerful tone, she introduces herself.

"Hello, I am Roza. I brought you refreshments—the cheese blintzes are homemade. Coffee and soda are over there. Enjoy," she says, putting down the tray on the nearby counter.

"Thank you, precious," Shlomo responds with an affectionate smile.

"You're welcome. I am going for a swim now," Roza replies.

"Well, well—have fun." Shlomo affectionately blows her a kiss.

"Thank you, bubala [*sweetie*]. You know I will."

"My wife Roza is an aquatic veterinarian. She has a wild dolphin that needs intensive attention after surgery—more than an aquatic trainer can provide. Part of the attention is swimming with Delphi—that's her name—a couple of times daily. That's why we have a saltwater aquarium."

"Oh," Olivia says as if she meets people like that every day. The truth is that Shlomo and Roza are a most unusual and intriguing couple.

"Okay, are we ready?" the Rav asks while rolling up his sleeves and rubbing his hands together. Leading the way, first, he gets himself a cup of coffee and two cheese blintzes.

The three spend all afternoon together exploring, discussing, and clarifying Olivia's problems. In the end, all agree on five concerns with potential solutions to guide the conversation. The Rav summarizes them as follows:

"Firstly, you no longer know what is real or unreal. We propose that reality is shaped by consensus."

"Secondly, you are afraid of going insane. We propose that sanity is more important than normalcy."

"Thirdly, you don't understand why you wake up in dreams where you meet Uri and experience past lives. We propose that our past lives can teach us lessons about the dynamics of relationships."

"Fourthly, you have no clue what a soul or soulmate is. We propose that souls start as primal essences that can manifest in other bodies or forms.

"Fifthly, you don't understand why Uri thinks he is your soulmate. We propose that one may or may not get to know their soulmates."

"Is that list comprehensive enough so we can start working?" the Rav asks Olivia.

"I think that's it," Olivia replies, placing her hope in the logical process.

"Excellent!" the Rav claps his hands three times.

Uri joins in the clapping. "Yeah, we're getting somewhere!"

"Very well, let's have a break and then get right to it. If needed, we can tweak the list as we go."

CHAPTER NINE

Consensus Shapes Reality

During the break, the Rav asks Uri and Olivia if they want to meet Delphi. They do. The Rav leads the way as they step outside. Roza is in the pool dressed in a black wetsuit with a front zipper. She waves her right hand and shouts, "Come in, come in the water!"

"We don't have swimsuits," Olivia objects.

"Just jump in. You can always change into robes later while we throw your clothes in the dryer," the Rav encourages them.

"Really?" Olivia and Uri ask at the same time.

"Really," the Rav answers, setting the example. He takes off his sandals and beret, places them on a lounge chair, and dives fully clothed into the pool.

They learn that Delphi has had surgery after injuries from a boat propeller that almost killed her. Roza shows them the scars and explains what type of physical therapy she has been doing with Delphi, who will be ready to permanently move into the Clearwater Marine Aquarium in a week or two.

After enjoying themselves in the water and swimming a few laps near Delphi, they get out with wet clothes clinging to their bodies. Then they briefly rinse off under an outside shower before walking into the house.

Back inside, the Rav leads them to the bathroom. There, they dry off with fresh towels and put on white waffle robes. After that, they return to the office and work on Olivia's problem number one: Not knowing what is real or not. The Rav begins with, "Let's explore the hypothesis that reality is shaped by consensus. Of course, we can agree or disagree with each other, but we must present arguments that can be further examined for validity. Needless to say, personal experience matters in reaching a consensus. But if we can't produce any evidence, then we have to find another way to help Olivia."

"How would that be of use to me?" Olivia asks.

"Remember, you no longer know what is real," Uri reminds her.

"Yes, and if we can personally relate to you by having experienced living in a past life, it might also be possible to wake up in a dream to it," the Rav adds.

"Perhaps it would help to see how consensus reality works by looking at a simple example," Uri suggests.

"Agreed, that might help," Olivia nods.

"Okay, describe what you see," the Rav holds up a pen.

"A pen," Uri and Olivia respond in unison.

"What else do you see?"

"It's black," Olivia replies.

"It's thick," Uri adds.

"Okay, we're getting somewhere. All of us agree that this is a pen. But is it true that it is black? What if I tell you that it's a very dark blue?"

"I'd have to look closer," Olivia admits.

"How about the thickness?" The Rav takes a thicker pen and holds it up against the first one.

"I previously made a statement that was based on not having seen the other one," Uri acknowledges.

"Very good. While there are questions as to the color and thickness of the pen, we all agree that this is a pen, right?"

Uri and Olivia nod their heads.

"Therefore, our consensus is that this is a pen. But that's only because we speak English. In another language, a pen might be called something different. Do we also have a consensus on what the pen is used for?"

"Perhaps—unless it is used only for a specific task— like a black pen might be required for government documentation."

"Yes, but the bottom line is that we all agree that this is a pen we can write, scribble, or draw with, and that establishes our functional reality for it."

Olivia and Uri agree.

"Now, let's look at this setting. We have bought into everything we see as our common reality—shelves, books, a desk, table, chairs, Keurig, SodaStream Fizzy—even the walls and the house itself."

Uri and Olivia's eyes scan the room.

"There is no doubt about it, but what does that have to do with me waking up in my dreams?" Olivia asks.

"Well, the entire world knows that when we go to sleep, we dream. However, some people don't know that there is psychological evidence that if we can predict recurring nightmares, we can teach ourselves to wake up while we're having them. So, our question is if we can wake up in a dream in a past life? As a prerequisite, we'd have to establish that the metaphysical is a pre-existing and continuing reality. Individuals from Hindu and Buddhist cultures believe just that."

"Who in this room does?" Olivia questions.

"I don't rule it out, being fully aware that it sounds just as ridiculous as the beliefs that prophet Elijah never died and shows up in different human forms to test people. And, for whom many families reserve a seat by the table during Passover—just in case he returns—in which case the world as we know is ending."

"Or the Christian dogma related to the immaculate conception, trinity, or resurrection of Christ," Roza adds.

"I don't rule it out. Either it's all true—at least for some people on developmental levels—or it's all nonsense," Uri asserts.

"So where is the evidence of our own experiences?" the Rav questions.

"When I met Olivia, I knew that I had met her before in the Ottoman Empire as Jakuv and that we were soulmates," Uri responds.

"As for me, when working with Dr. Blackwood, the regression psychiatrist, I discovered that, among other lives, I had previously lived as Ragnar Lodbrok, the Viking King, in the ninth century," the Rav discloses.

"And I learned that I was Bishop Christian the First in the eleventh century who had a harem and under whose auspices the Scharfenstein Castle in Kiedrich, Hesse was built," Roza chimes in upon entering the room.

Because such disclosures can be shocking to someone just beginning to deal with transmigration, an anticipatory silence fills the room. All eyes are on Olivia. The tension arising from these outrageous claims is written all over her face.

"I find this disturbing," she says with a frown.

"Why?"

"Because Kiedrich is on the other side of the Atlantic. It's where I grew up!"

"Really?" Roza was surprised.

"Yes." The tower of that castle on a steep hill and the open courtyard is the only thing still standing. It's surrounded by vineyards, and I was part of many of the village festivities taking place up there. The castle was built in 1160 CE by Christian I, the Archbishop of Mainz. I learned to view it as a monument bearing witness to the oppression of the villagers by Roman robber barons who burdened them with heavy taxes. Today, many villagers take pride in their Gothic roots."

To build rapport, the Rav reveals bits of his knowledge about the history of the world Olivia came from. "Yes, when enemy forces like the Vikings—my people from a past life—or Huns did not overrun the Germanic tribes, they were fiercely fighting among themselves. Later, after the King of the Ostrogoth's Theodore the Great besieged Rom, he became the first Barbarian King of Italy. And after that, the Germanic tribes became a mostly united and mixed Romanized barbarian people—like Roza when she lived at Bishop Christian I.

"But back to your recent experiences, Olivia. As long as you continue to meet your day-to-day obligations such as generating an income, paying bills, and caring for yourself and your loved ones—whose business is it that you have experienced past lives?"

"Exactly. Besides worrying about your sanity—granted, that's important to keep. But what have you lost so far?" Uri challenges her.

"Nothing," Olivia admits.

"And what have you gained?' Roza's face shows curiosity.

"I guess an additional perspective." Olivia scratches her head.

"That's very good," Roza compliments her.

The Rav continues with a lecture.

"Let's consider the far-out religious beliefs of various subcultures that are alive and well today. While they are considered normal, they are not necessarily sane. I don't have to mention them by name. Interestingly, even when people discard their subcultural beliefs as nonsense, they often become complicit by looking the other way when their leaders conduct the worst of atrocities. Societal mores are constantly fluctuating to protect powerful ruling castes."

"I don't quite understand. Would you please provide some examples?" Olivia asks.

"Sure, complicity is the problem because it normalizes horrific events. It made it possible that millions of *undesirables* were murdered in extermination camps and gas chambers by the Nazis. It ensured that millions of *enemies* were sent slave labor to the gulags by the Marxists. And it keeps in place the suffering of the *untouchables* in India by intentionally not aiding them. Even today, complicity with Middle Eastern terrorists and their disciples wreak havoc with suicide missions and beheadings."

"Yes, but what about right in our backyard?" Uri challenges him. "We have all these riots where people get hurt or killed. Something is very wrong when African Americans constitute only 12% of our society but make up 50% of our prison population?"

The Rav counters, "Yet, we *are* making progress. We have learned that allowing social conflict is necessary to break the destructive bonds of complicity. Only that allows the emergence of new bonds to pursue healthy social interest within a framework of unity that respects diversity."

Roza chimes in, "Yes, because of the separation of church and state, we have no need to label far-out beliefs as psychotic or force others to believe *nothing*. The United States is a young country with a promising future. The colonial *storming* phase against old European castes has made room to *forming* new ways of doing things to relieve oppression and *norming* the previously impossible—like electing a black president. And, as long as we fulfill our obligation to Uncle Sam, who cares?"

"As far as reality goes, why can't we just accept that even a so-called opposing perspective can be part of the same coin? So, for example, a pen is still a pen in English spelled from left to right, but an *et* in Hebrew spelled from right to left," the Rav questions.

"And even if the people of an illiterate culture only use pens to keep their hair in place, then *that's* normal for them," Uri comments.

"Actually, I have a coworker who uses pencils for that exact purpose. She has multicultural skills," Olivia adds with half-hearted laughter.

Now, everyone else joins in the laughter while Olivia is reminded of the sound of the Shofar in the dine-in theater and the letters populating from right to left.

"Let's summarize what we've learned so far. Reality is forged by a consensus of people making deliberate or unconscious decisions based on what they agree on. What does it matter as long as it doesn't interfere with love, work, and life generally? In fact, it seems beneficial to have shared realities with as many people as we can. So far, we have established that all four of us have had past life experiences. Therefore, we agree that past lives are possible. What are your thoughts, Olivia?"

"I can live with that." Olivia breathes with a sigh of relief.

She decides that the Rav makes sense. He and his wife admitted having explored their own past lives, and Uri has shared his experiences as well. This leaves her feeling validated. The undesirable alternative is the psych ward in order to get squeezed into standards of living with mental illness. And there is no way that she is willing to go that route.

"Thank you all, but, just the same, I think I will stop waking up in my dreams to past lives now—just like some people learn how to stop their nightmares by waking up," she announces.

"That is perfectly okay," the Rav reassures her with a smile.

"I have absolutely no problems with that either," Uri adds.

The time has come to leave. By now, Uri and Olivia's clothes have dried, and they take turns changing in the bathroom. While the Rav escorts them to the front door, he leaves them with the following.

"By the way, did you know that that General Patton experienced previous lives in battle, such as having been Roman legionnaire and soldier in the 14th century Bohemian Army?"

"Wow—that's amazing," Uri replies.

Olivia feels too tired to respond. All she wants is to go home. To forget about walking up past lives for a while and get a good night's sleep. During the ride home, she can barely keep her eyes open. Uri parks at her house. He follows her in. She doesn't care and walks straight to the bedroom. She takes off her shoes and crawls in her bed with her clothes on. Uri covers her gently with the comforter and kisses her on the cheek. Then she drifts off.

CHAPTER TEN

Higher Than Heaven

After a couple of days have passed, Olivia feels rejuvenated. She decides to try it again. The chant *Wake up in my dream* still works. As before, Olivia finds herself in the dine-in movie theater. On the screen, white letters form the words *Into the Future* against a starry sky. Melodies of Jewish nigunim, religious songs expressing a joy using sounds, fill the atmosphere.

> *Bim-Bam, Bim-Bam, Bim-Bam, Bim-Bam.*
> *Lai-Lai-Lai-Lai, Lai-Lai-Lai-Lai, Lai-Lai-Lai Lai,*
> *Lai-Lai Lai.*
> *Bim-Bam, Bim-Bam, Bim-Bam, Bim-Bam.*

Her heart flutters as Uri walks in. As in the past, they mutually brush cheeks with light kisses. "Olivia—I am so happy to see you again! How are you?"

Feeling appreciated, Olivia responds, "I am okay, thanks for asking. How about you?"

"Oh, good. But I missed you, and now I feel even better knowing you are well. Today you'll experience glimpses a special type of gilgul, which means wheel, and stands for soul transmigration. As such, it is closely tied to an individual having relieved a specific quota of suffering for others while on earth. By reaching that quota, the scales of justice are tipped in that individual's favor. As a result, they are free from the cycle of rebirth as other humans, animals, plants, and inanimate objects."

Before Olivia can respond, a loud "Bim-Bam" is followed by the white letters and black sky forming a moving spiral. Unable to resist, Olivia feels herself pulled into a starry future.

She softly lands in a field projecting translucent multicolored bands connected to a multitude of people at a reception. Some look familiar, others she has never seen before. All bodies, including her own, are joined by the bands. Olivia feels deeply connected to everyone around her. She not only sees colors but also touches them. She not only hears sounds but also sees them. And she not only feels emotions but also hears and sees them. Olivia recognizes that she is experiencing a neuropsychological phenomenon called synesthesia that she had learned about in a psychology class. The people around her radiate joy accompanied by frequent giggles or laughs. The loving interactions are tied to an all-transcending, gently loving, pulsating source. *Is synesthesia what the Israelites experienced at Mount Sinai when they saw the sounds?*

Suddenly, Olivia spots her parents. *Could this be real?* They had died in a car accident two years ago. Their bodies are connected to the bands reaching deep into Olivia's essence. They approach her with open arms and smiles. Her mother takes her face into her hands, examines it, kisses her, and says lovingly, "My Olivia, I missed you so much, but now you are finally here."

Her parents join her in a group hug. United, they laugh and cry tears of joy while taking turns examining each other. As they separate, Olivia notices that the color bands connecting them are flexible and stretch according to their distance. She also sees her brother and grandparents, uncles, aunts, cousins, and countless others.

Suddenly, a beautiful woman appears whose head is partially covered by an Ottoman cap with an attached silk scarf. She looks vaguely familiar and is flanked by two couples. "Olivia!" the woman shouts as the rays of the rainbow connect them.

"Who are you?"

"I am you—Miriam, from your past life," the woman explains.

"That's incredible! Why am I you?"

"I was reincarnated in your lifetime as you, Olivia, to relieve suffering one more time for someone else to end my cycle of rebirth." She takes off her cap and hands it to Olivia. "Remember when you wore this in the Topkapi Palace?"

Olivia accepts her old headgear, holds it in her hands, and responds, "Yes, yes. I remember now from waking up in my dream. But where are we now in the process of having relieved suffering?"

"Congratulations! You did it. That's why we are in Higher-Than-Heaven."

"Really? How did I do it?"

"For now, you just need to know that you played an important part in successfully alleviating the suffering of many people. Because of the butterfly effect of one action leading to another, the scales of justice tipped in your favor and pushed you into a new existence. Alex will explain it to you later."

"Who is Alex?"

"You will know soon. But first, look at your parents from the Ottoman Empire." Miriam points to the two couples. "Here are my birth parents, and there are my adoptive parents. Because you lived as me before, all of my parents are also yours."

Olivia recognizes them at once. There is no room for doubt; she remembers having seen the kind and smiling faces before. Her ancestral parents wear the typical 15th Century Karaite Jewish ethnic outfits and her adoptive ones the Greek Orthodox ones as was customary during her past life experience. The reunion is accompanied by warm embraces, kisses, and happy laughter.

As the quadruple fades into the background, Olivia's previous self, Miriam, approaches her again. This time, she holds the hand of a woman whose red hair is topped by the pointed headgear of an ottoman queen and adorned with jewels on her forehead. Olivia recognizes her as her adoptive sister Aleksandra, aka Hurrem.

"Aleksandra!" "Miriam!" the sisters shout and fall into each other's arms, laughing and crying at the same time. Finally, the suffering from being ripped from their families and subsequent subjugation as slaves is reconciled by an equal measure of joy. Everyone is reunited, and thoughts of their oppressors only serve like thorns adorning bushes of multicolored thriving roses.

But what about Jakuv, the jeweler, and Kismet, the eunuch? Where do they fit in? And where is Uri? As Olivia ponders, all three show up in a group accompanied by— Mickey Blackstone!

With a mischievous smile, Uri points to Jakuv, saying, "He is me."

Jakuv points back at him, countering, "And he is me!"

Likewise, Kismet points to Mickey. "He is me."

Mickey points back at him. "And he is me!" Subsequently, people around burst out laughing and joined in pointing and identifying each other. "He is me," "She is me," and "They are me," and the like.

Olivia is stunned. "How do *you* fit into all of that?" she asks Mickey.

He explains, "After his castration, Atanas became the eunuch Kismet at the Topkapi Palace but reincarnated as me later. At one point, it was all over the news that my father had me chemically castrated when I was 11years old to preserve my voice and get rid of acne. The fact is that everyone made money off me from when I was a little boy until I finally overdosed on propofol and benzodiazepines. And that ended my existence as a pop star on earth."

"Yes, but you also were the most philanthropic pop star in history, giving over 300 million dollars to charity and saving countless lives," Kismet adds.

Mickey responds with clear admiration. "And you started the first functional support group for eunuchs in the Ottoman Empire. As Kismet, you saved thousands of boys who would have otherwise died. After they were either kidnapped or sold by their parents, the future for those who survived castration looked grim, even if they entered religious life or vernacular theaters. You rescued countless of them from a life of degradation as prostitutes until dying in the gutters by getting them involved in the coffee trade with your friend Adom from Egypt."

To which Kismet answers, "After Hurrem set me free, I knew I had to do something. Unlike the complete removal of the genital apparatus, these boys only had their testicles crushed or removed before puberty to keep their voices from breaking to take the place of females who were forbidden to sing in public. The Golden Age of the Castrati had not arrived yet with producing stars like Farinelli as sopranos for the opera and even Sistine Chapel—when the mob in Italy would openly scream, "Long live the knife!"

As Olivia ponders what suffering she might have alleviated in the past, other than saving Hurrem from drowning herself when on the slave ship, a familiar-looking man accompanied by what appears to be his mother and father arrive. "Remember us?" the woman asks with a smile. You came to our house as a mobile therapist and saved our family. And for that, we are forever grateful!"

Olivia had completely forgotten about that period in her life. Then, as part of an interdisciplinary team, she had worked with Alex, a six-year-old boy with an autism spectrum disorder. Alex had developed the grotesque habit of violently humping and punching stuffed animals but could not verbally express why. After his behavior had come to the attention of the pre-school teacher, he filed an abuse report with Family Services. As a mandated reporter of child abuse, the teacher suspected that Alex was either experiencing or witnessing violent sexual abuse. From that point on, key staff involved in Alex's wrap-around social services were looking for evidence to remove him from his home.

While gathering information for her assessment, studying his records, meeting with his parents, and spending time alone with him, Olivia noticed an innocent smile on his face awkwardly turned towards her when humping and beating his teddy bear. That's when it dawned on her that Alex was looking for approval. The breakthrough came when she spoke to the parents about their evening routine and bedtime. The truth was that Alex pretended to be a show-wrestler—like the ones he was allowed to watch with his dad before going to bed.

"You're the only one who gave us the benefit of the doubt," says the father while the mother nods her head.

Alex proudly adds, "Yes, because you mobilized the national leaders of Mental Health Services, I became a network engineer for Mental Health Services Global instead of ending up in a dead-end facility. I could have never done that alone with my parents' limited knowledge and resources. With the experts testifying on my behalf, my future started moving in the right direction. As a result of winning a lawsuit, I was able to get into Marshall University, where I majored in Computer Science. That's where I developed my expertise in coding software and learning the scripting languages for automation and cloud orchestration.

"Well, as a social worker, it was my job to create macro-level interventions if needed to help someone, and I am so—" Before Olivia could finish her sentence, Mickey dances up to Alex in the moonwalk step. They fist-bump, laugh, and take turns pointing at each other and themselves. Mickey starts. "He is also me."

Alex responds, "And I am he."

"But you both lived around the same time on the earth time. How is that possible?" Olivia questions.

"The overlapping existence was possible because I am on the spectrum, Alex replies. "I am connected to others in ways that tie to the fields of transmission genetic, epigenetic, and environmental factors. In that respect, my perception and functioning are unique and unexplainable to the ordinary mind. But I can vouch for Mickey's innocence like you vouched for my parents. He never abused any children at Neverplace. His love for them came from an undefiled place and was pure. The media worked hard to ruin his reputation to increase their ratings.

Alex's words make sense, and Olivia has no further questions. Now she understands what Miriam meant with the butterfly effect of one action leading to another and the scales of justice tipping in her favor and pushing her into a new existence. As a result, she has spiraled into a world that lacks space for the scales of judgment and only shows rectification. The veil has lifted. V*e-a-hav-ta* *le-re-a-cha ka-mo-cha.* She grasps that one soul dressed in various bodies has practiced the ancient mandate *Love Your Neighbor as Yourself.* Not *like* but *as* until a particular reincarnation alleviates their specific share of suffering and creates a corresponding responding level of joy. She gets it. Upon achieving justice due to the accumulated effect of acts by multiple persons, the need to reincarnate once more has become obsolete.

Meanwhile, a funeral takes place on earth for Olivia's body separated from her essence. "We, therefore, commit this body to the ground, earth to earth, ashes to ashes, dust to dust…." And no one at the funeral, including her husband Joe, has a clue that she has transmigrated to Higher-Than-Heaven.

CHAPTER ELEVEN

Before Meeting Uri

The clock at her bedside shows 6:00 AM. Joe is already up. Awake, Olivia feels relieved from the tension of fleeting memories. "Ah," she sighs with relief but can't help wondering if she might have woken up to her own daytime nightmare instead of from sleep. "Nonsense," she firmly tells herself. "It will get better." All necessary precautions have been taken. Joe is back home on leave, in therapy for PTSD, learns to live without performance-enhancing steroids, and sleeps in the guest room.

"Well, I-I'm a sucker for fine Cuban cigars...." Joe bellows Fred Paisley's *Cigar Song* from the direction of the master bathroom. She is glad that he has returned from active combat in one piece. While his physical injuries have healed, the nightmares and a changed personality tell a different story. It has become dangerous for them to sleep in the same bed because of his hypervigilance and involuntary startle reflexes. During Operation Moshtarak, his helicopter was downed by hostile fire. Subsequently, he had been captured by the Taliban, who started a violent interrogation despite his injuries. Fortunately, he had been rescued by a coalition of Afghan-US forces fairly quickly.

During the next couple of days, Olivia feels a renewed sense of hope. Preoccupied with Joe's needs and her daily business, Olivia gets angry when people confuse clinical social workers with welfare caseworkers who snatch little kids away and break up families. She is licensed to assess, diagnose, and provide therapy to help patients improve their lives. Today, she has four appointments.

But first, both Olivia and Joe have a glass of enriched water. After that, they run for 30 minutes on the Pinellas Trail. Back home, she makes fresh smoothies. Then they take showers, get dressed, and go for a big breakfast at Tiffany's. After breakfast, they part ways. Olivia thought that things were going fairly well—until he informs her that he is cleared for re-deployment. It's not up for debate. Back to Afghanistan. Back to fighting the Taliban and Al-Qaeda. Back to leaving her behind, without hope that anything could ever change for the better.

Her first appointment is with Jim, a 50-year-old double leg amputee with phantom pains and a high anxiety level. He lives in his own home and has home health services. His goal is to get a special wheelchair that allows him to move through sand. Jim is quite open about wanting to enjoy the beach and and watching pretty girls in bikinis

Her second appointment is with Nilda, a 39-year-old female who is bedridden because of advanced symptoms of Multiple Sclerosis. After her husband abandoned her, she moved in with her older sister. Mostly lethargic and depressed, Nilda enjoys listening to Eddie Palmieri, the finest pianist and "madman" of Latin Jazz. She wants to improve her mood and increase her physical activity.

The third appointment is with Mike, a 35-year-old male resident in an Assisted Living Facility who struggles with complicated grief. His girlfriend died during a car accident he caused while under the influence of alcohol. He sustained one-sided paralysis and speech impairment from irreversible neurological brain damage. In addition to feeling depressed, Mike is haunted by massive guilt from which he seeks relief.

Her final appointment is with Jackie, a 73-year-old married female who keeps seeing frogs in the house, including inside water bottles in the refrigerator. Olivia is no longer sure that she hallucinates. Instead, she suspects that her husband is placing them to drive her insane for his own reasons.

All of her clients suffer from serious trauma. Despite knowing that her work put her at risk for secondary traumatic stress and vicarious trauma, Olivia's coping strategy over the years had been avoidance to consider that possibility.

In the dim light of the moon, Olivia feels pinned under his 240 pounds of weight. She gasps for air as Joe's hands tighten around her neck. "Stop it… Stop it… I'm Olivia… Wake up…." She hears herself croak while struggling to break free. Joe is having a psychotic episode. Suddenly, his body turns limp and rolls to the side.

Olivia draws in a deep breath. It was another failed attempt to sleep in the same bed. Again, Joe has mistaken her for the enemy. Covering his head with both hands, he moans, "Oh my God, I'm home. What have I done…." But Olivia is far from being safe. She has moved too close to the edge of the bed. When she hits the floor, her head slams against a footstool.

CHAPTER TWELVE

In the Hospital

The chant *Wake up in my dream* still works. As before, Olivia finds herself in the dine-in movie theater. On the screen, white letters form the words *Into the Future* against a starry sky. Melodies of nigunim lamenting physical pain with sounds fill the atmosphere.

> *Bim-Bam, Bim-Bam, Bim-Bam, Bim-Bam.*
> *Yai-Yai-Yai-Yai,   Yai-Yai-Yai-Yai,   Yai-Yai-Yai-Yai,*
> *Yai-Yai-Yai-Yai.*
> *Bim-bam, Bim-Bam, Bim-Bam, Bim-Bam.*

At the precise ending of a loud "Bim-Bam," the white letters and black sky turn into a moving spiral, and Olivia feels herself pulled into a starry future. She is landing in a bed. A pillow props up her back. Her eyes are opening. A needle on the top of her right hand intravenously connects to a bag of fluids. Her gaze falls on a large whiteboard across from her on the wall. The writing with a black marker shows the medications, dosages, and times due.

Slightly to the left is a computer on a stand. Further left is an open door. The wall to her right has a large window with an empty windowsill. A TV is mounted near the left corner. Her head hurts. She touches it with her left hand and feels that it is wrapped in a thick bandage.

I am in the hospital! How did I get here? As Olivia remembers bits and pieces of otherworldly experiences, a nurse enters the room.

"Hi, I'm glad to see you awake. My name is Evelyn, your nurse for the shift," she says with a smile. And, as if reading Olivia's mind, she adds, "You are in the ICU because you had grand mal seizures and lost consciousness. It seems like you also had an older head injury that was never treated because you still have a big bump on your head. The color of it shows that it's not new. You already had a CT scan but also need an MRI. The neurologist will be in to talk to you later. If you need help, just press the button."

Except for her name, Olivia can't remember anything about her actual life before her admission. The neurologist informs her that her provisional diagnosis is dissociative amnesia due to a TBI, short for traumatic brain injury.

Then she loses consciousness again. And no one at the hospital has a clue where she is, even though they see her body and monitor her vitals.

CHAPTER THIRTEEN

Where is Oliva?

The chant *Wake up in my dream* still works. As before, Olivia finds herself in the dine-in movie theater. On the screen, white letters form the words *Into the Future* against a starry sky. Melodies of nigunim lamenting distress with sounds fill the atmosphere.

> *Bim-Bam, Bim-Bam, Bim-Bam, Bim-Bam.*
> *Aai-Aai-Aai-Aai, Aai-Aai-Aai-Aai, Aai-Aai-Aai-Aai, Aai-Aai-Aai-Aai.*
> *Bim-Bam, Bim-Bam, Bim-Bam, Bim-Bam.*

At the precise ending of a loud "Bim-Bam," the white letters and black sky turn into a moving spiral, and Olivia feels herself pulled into the future.

Landing in a chair, her eyes open though she feels overly drowsy as if medicated. She finds herself sitting in a circle with other women and men. She notices that all the furniture in the room—tables, chairs, and shelves—is manufactured from heavy plastic and screwed to the floor.

A huge window is barred from the outside. No one wears shoelaces or belts.

One woman's appearance suggests a special status. She wears a white coat and gold-rimmed designer glasses fastened to a decorative chain. Her legs are crossed, a legal pad rests on her right knee, and her hand rests on it holding a pen. "My name is Helga. I'm your group therapist," she says with a friendly smile. "Today's topic is 'Active Coping Strategies.' Let's see what we already know and then learn a couple of new skills. But first things first, let's introduce our newest group member."

Now looking directly at her, Helga raises her voice, "Welcome to our group, Olivia. Perhaps you can tell us briefly why you are here and anything else you want us to know." All eyes stare at her. They are eager to hear whatever she will disclose about herself to either provide genuine support or use the knowledge against her later, depending on their personality disturbances and motives.

"No—don't—remember—nothing—nothing—don't—anything," Olivia responds accompanied by rigid gestures. Her voice is monotonous and affect flat. Suddenly, she utters, "Away—away," accompanied by a bizarre salute.

During the next clinical team meeting, Helga mentions that "In group, Olivia had that look like no one is home." Promptly, the supervising psychiatrist directs her to use proper clinical language. Next, he models the listing of Olivia's cluster of symptoms, indicating a provisional diagnosis of catatonic schizophrenia related to a TBI.

Then Olivia loses consciousness again. And no one at the psychiatric unit has a clue where she is—even though they see her body and monitor her vitals.

CHAPTER 14

Integration

While undergoing additional tests and assessments, Olivia slowly regains enough cognition and memory to provide her biopsychosocial information. The medical team agrees that she has suffered from a previously untreated TBI, seizures, loss of consciousness, brain swelling, and finally a coma.

When the nurse gives Olivia a heads up that Dr. Fielding from neuroscience is about to make his rounds, Olivia is fully awake. She knows who she is, and much of her memory has returned. Shortly after, a tall man in a white coat enters, followed by a group of interns. He introduces himself and starts to examine her. After exchanging medical terminology with the interns, Dr. Fielding tells her the following:

"Falling out of the bed and hitting your head was the catalyst setting in motion your loss of consciousness and near-death experiences. During your coma, you experienced states of depressed consciousness. That allowed your brain to heal because your cerebral hemispheres no longer interacted with the area of your brainstem called the reticular activating system. During that state, the EEGs of your brain showed no signs of a sleep-wakeful cycle. Therefore, it is impossible that you were dreaming then."

While Dr. Fielding offers his medical explanations, he does not provide Olivia with fully satisfying information. Later, another physician comes to see her. He introduces himself as Dr. Goldman, a middle-aged psychiatrist with round spectacles, who provides further clarification:

"Even during periods of consciousness, you struggled with being alert, attentive, and oriented. Your state of mind moved heavily between the drowsiness of theta and deep sleep of delta. Because you had lost the concept of sequential time, actual events got distorted and entangled with memories, thoughts acquired by learning, and ongoing subconscious processes of your mind."

Despite the answers from both doctors, Olivia can't help wondering about her Higher-Than-Heaven experience with accompanying synesthesia. That's why she decides to request a visit by a hospital chaplain. She is pleasantly surprised when a petite slim woman with mid-length brown hair covered by a kippah enters her room.

"Hello, Olivia. My name is Rabbi Melka Chinsky. I am trained in clinical pastoral counseling," she says confidently with a warm smile. "Call me Melka. How are you?"

"Getting better, thank you, Rabbi. But my near-death experiences have left me with all these questions coming from deep within. And my marriage is over because I have to break a trauma bond to get well. My heart is aching for answers." Olivia sighs heavily.

"I already had a consult with the medical team," the Rabbi replies." So go ahead, tell me whatever you want. Perhaps we can find some answers by putting our heads together."

"You really think so?"

"Sure, there is a solution for every problem, including what you are struggling with. I am convinced of that. Where is your husband now?"

"Back in Afghanistan with the 82nd Airborne Division. On his third tour as fighter pilot captain."

"I see. We can deal with your marital problems later. I strongly recommend ongoing psychotherapy to help you sort out matters after discharge. And you can also call me anytime," the rabbi states, handing her a colorful business card emblazoned by a Star of David. But first, let's deal with your near-death experiences.

Feeling encouraged, Olivia pours out her heart while the rabbi engages in active listening without judgement.

She waits until Olivia is done before she responds. "First, I want to thank you for your confidence in me, Olivia. I feel honored. I studied your medical chart. This world is a narrow bridge, and you almost fell off. But we're glad to have you back. The important thing for you is to embrace now because that is all we ever really have. Memories of the past and projections into the future are only useful when they can help us to better cope in the present. You can certainly learn from your subjective experiences. But they do not it into our objective reality—as does anyone's near-death accounts. But instead of giving you advice, I think you might benefit from an extended-comparison parable using figure of speech with hidden meanings that your mind can use to organize itself. Would you like to hear it?"

"Sure, at this point, I appreciate anything that might help me make sense of my experiences—in addition to what I heard from the doctors."

"Great, you got what you needed from the best medical professionals. I hope you gain an added perspective from the ancient parable I modified to benefit women. It is about twins in a womb having a conversation. But first, I want to clarify that it has nothing to do with the current pro-life versus pro-choice initiatives. You can share the earliest belief of rabbis that a fetus is a limb of the woman until it takes its first breath or that it is fully human at an earlier point. Either way, I believe you can benefit from my gender-specific version that ends with a girl instead of a boy."

"I'm glad you clarified that, and I look forward to hearing it."

The Rabbi begins.

Imagine twins having a conversation in the womb. Both experience their physical space getting tighter by the day but have different expectations for the future.

One of the twins is a rationalist who argues, 'Life in the womb here is all there is until we die.'

The other one can't accept having all these growing organs for no future purpose and responds, 'I believe in a world to come where I can use my eyes, mouth, nose, arms, and legs.'

'Nonsense,' replies the first twin. 'No one can ever survive without the umbilical cord. It's the supply pipe that provides us with needed oxygen and nutrients in the placenta and removes waste. We're safe only as long as we are in the sack of fluid. When you leave the womb, you die. You better believe it.'

'I can't—although I have no idea what might come. Still, there must be something greater than this womb out there, or we wouldn't even think about it. And sometimes I hear sounds and see shadows that seem to come from elsewhere than here.'

Both continue to argue while bumping into each other, moved by contractions increasing frequency and strengths. Suddenly, during an especially violent contraction, the one with the faith begins to be pushed out of the birth canal. Now the rationalist is sure that his sibling's life has come to its end. It is exactly happening as he predicted. That seems confirmed by the faint cries heard from a distance. Horrified at what just happened, he feels helpless and abandoned.

Yet, on the other side, there is a warm welcome by many caring hands accompanied by the words, 'It's a girl!'

"I wonder if they ever stopped arguing after both were born?" Olivia asks.

"That's a good question. What do you think?" The Rabbi laughs.

"I know that Joe keeps bumping into me. What do I do?"

"Don't waste your energy fighting him, trying to change him or anyone else. Use the energy of the struggle to blaze your own path."

"Hmm."

"No matter what, have faith in your destiny."

###

In rehab after her inpatient hospitalization, Olivia finds herself in similar situations as her past clients. Physical therapy, psychotherapy, case management, and ongoing medical treatment—now it's *her* turn to get it all. Occasionally, Melka drops in for a meaningful chat. As Olivia focuses on her daily rehab schedule, memories of her other-worldly experiences fade. She starts feeling more hopeful about her future. Among sporadic visits from relatives and friends, even Sandy and Fred came to see her. But she has not heard from Joe, which worries her.

One day, Joe's mother, her two friends, and Melka show up at the same time. Everyone is somber, and her mother-in-law is crying. She feels a knot forming in the pit of her stomach accompanied by lightheadedness. Before anyone tells her, she knows. It had happened near Kabul while she was in a coma. Joe had been at the wrong place at the wrong time. A seemingly lost child had approached their camp but was on a suicide mission. According to religious tradition, Joe's body had been laid to rest before sundown upon its return to the United States.

Despite being surrounded by people who care, Olivia feels a numb sense of abandonment. She can't help wondering about what Joe's last moments might have been. *What a way to go, away from all the people who cared about him. It is not fair that he left without saying goodbye. That I had no say as to the outcome of our relationship. That they had a funeral without me. That I have no clue where he is. Does anyone ever really have a say when the time comes to leave—or to return? Who knows, I might be with Joe in a past or future that I am unaware of right now….*

Three years have passed. Olivia is able to work again. Her relationship with Melka has taken on a new dimension. In addition to their daily work that pays the bills, they travel, hold workshops, and author books. Their mission is to relieve suffering, to validate the shades of gray of subjective experiences, and to repair the damages of binary of crazy or sane judgements. They effectively help people all over the world to explore and make sense of their own metaphysical or near-death experiences.

Wherever Uri might be—if there is one, Olivia no longer misses him or his sparkling green eyes. And in whatever world Joe might smoke his Cuban cigars now, she wishes him well. Melka is more than enough. Her brown eyes glow with the warmth of an everlasting hearth, tenderness, and wisdom. Unless she gets angry, then she pitches a fit. That's when Olivia steps in and shines by deescalating her. After all, she is a therapist.

The End

EPILOGUE

A nd no one knows where he is…. Classical science has not yet discovered a location for consciousness. Therefore, we humans continue to fight over whether or not there is a world to come. Even the ones with faith fight over how to get there—as if it is up to us to leave the womb. While on earth, could the solution be using emotional intelligence in order to unify inherently opposing forces as we have managed to do with electricity?

As experimental fiction, my story explores the metaphysical, reincarnation, and trauma in a way that lets readers develop their own insights and conclusions by providing alternate endings. Olivia's experiences result in a paradigm-shift of no longer viewing life as usual. One of my goals was to show how a traumatized person might integrate her subjective and objective experiences.

In my novella, medical, neuroscience, and clinical practitioners did their jobs. During the process, a female hospital chaplain steps in by modifying traditional wisdom to offer a contemporary and gender-specific solution.

ABOUT THE AUTHOR

M argrit Goodhand began creative writing during the 1980s. In 1988, she received the Jean Gray Allen Memorial Award, First Prize, for nonfiction from The Harrisburg Manuscript Club. After that, she completed college and graduate school and obtained post-graduate credentials in Clinical Social Work/Psychotherapy. Margrit is the author of *The AOVIA Principle: A Path of Unlimited Potential*. Additionally, she is the author of "Half An Amish Man" and "Rum and Coca Cola," two short stories published in *The Best of Dunedin Writers Group* anthologies.

Discussion Notes - Chapter One:

_____

_____

_____

_____

_____

_____

_____

_____

_____

_____

_____

Discussion Notes – Chapter Two:

Discussion Notes – Chapter Three:

Discussion Notes – Chapter Four:

Discussion Notes – Chapter Five:

Discussion Notes - Chapter Six:

Discussion Notes – Chapter Seven:

_____

_____

_____

_____

_____

_____

_____

_____

_____

_____

Discussion Notes – Chapter Eight:

_____

_____

_____

_____

_____

_____

_____

_____

_____

_____

_____

Discussion Notes – Chapter Nine:

Discussion Notes – Chapter Ten:

_____

_____

_____

_____

_____

_____

_____

_____

_____

_____

_____

Discussion Notes – Chapter Eleven:

Discussion Notes – Chapter Twelve:

_____

_____

_____

_____

_____

_____

_____

_____

_____

_____

_____

Discussion Notes – Chapter Thirteen:

_____

_____

_____

_____

_____

_____

_____

_____

_____

_____

Discussion Notes – Chapter Fourteen:

_____

_____

_____

_____

_____

_____

_____

_____

_____

_____

_____

Lightning Source UK Ltd.
Milton Keynes UK
UKHW012236161221
395788UK00002B/735